470L

PALM BEACH COUNTY
LIBRARY SYSTEM
3650 Summit Boulevard
West Palm Beach, FL 33406-4198

Dear Parents:

Congratulations! Your child is taking the first steps on an exciting journey. The destination? Independent reading!

STEP INTO READING® will help your child get there. The program offers five steps to reading success. Each step includes fun stories and colorful art or photographs. In addition to original fiction and books with favorite characters, there are Step into Reading Non-Fiction Readers, Phonics Readers and Boxed Sets, Sticker Readers, and Comic Readers—a complete literacy program with something to interest every child.

Learning to Read, Step by Step!

Ready to Read Preschool–Kindergarten
• big type and easy words • rhyme and rhythm • picture clues
For children who know the alphabet and are eager to begin reading.

Reading with Help Preschool–Grade 1
• basic vocabulary • short sentences • simple stories
For children who recognize familiar words and sound out new words with help.

Reading on Your Own Grades 1–3
• engaging characters • easy-to-follow plots • popular topics
For children who are ready to read on their own.

Reading Paragraphs Grades 2–3
• challenging vocabulary • short paragraphs • exciting stories
For newly independent readers who read simple sentences with confidence.

Ready for Chapters Grades 2–4
• chapters • longer paragraphs • full-color art
For children who want to take the plunge into chapter books but still like colorful pictures.

STEP INTO READING® is designed to give every child a successful reading experience. The grade levels are only guides; children will progress through the steps at their own speed, developing confidence in their reading. The F&P Text Level on the back cover serves as another tool to help you choose the right book for your child.

Remember, a lifetime love of reading starts with a single step!

Copyright © Anna E. Dewdney Literary Trust.
Copyright © 2019 Genius Brands International, Inc.

All rights reserved. Published in the United States by Random House Children's Books, a division of Penguin Random House LLC, New York. Originally published in hardcover in the United States by Penguin Young Readers, an imprint of Penguin Random House LLC, New York, in 2018.

Based on the Llama Llama series by Anna Dewdney

Step into Reading, Random House, and the Random House colophon are registered trademarks of Penguin Random House LLC.

Visit us on the Web!
StepIntoReading.com
rhcbooks.com

Educators and librarians, for a variety of teaching tools, visit us at
RHTeachersLibrarians.com

Library of Congress Cataloging-in-Publication Data is available upon request.
ISBN 978-0-593-43220-4 (trade) — ISBN 978-0-593-43221-1 (lib. bdg.)

Printed in the United States of America
10 9 8 7 6 5 4 3 2 1

This book has been officially leveled by using the F&P Text Level Gradient™ Leveling System.

Random House Children's Books supports the First Amendment and celebrates the right to read.

Penguin Random House LLC supports copyright. Copyright fuels creativity, encourages diverse voices, promotes free speech, and creates a vibrant culture. Thank you for buying an authorized edition of this book and for complying with copyright laws by not reproducing, scanning, or distributing any part in any form without permission. You are supporting writers and allowing Penguin Random House to publish books for every reader.

llama llama
loses a tooth

Anna Dewdney

based on the bestselling children's book series
by Anna Dewdney

Random House New York

Llama Llama carries a box

of his toys.

Mama Llama carries a box,

a bag, and a ball.

Crash!

"Sorry!" says Mama.

"I don't want to bump my loose tooth," says Llama.

He wants it to fall out on its own.

He will put it under his pillow.

Llama smiles at Mama.

"Oh no, Llama. Your tooth
already fell out!" Mama says.
But where did it go?

They remember the places they
visited that day—

Nelly Gnu's house, Luna Giraffe's
house, Daddy Gnu's bakery, and
the park.

Mama hugs Llama. "Don't worry.

We'll look here first," she says.

Mama shakes Llama's

bed blanket.

Llama plays
while they look.
They have fun.
But they don't find
Llama's tooth.

Next they look in the kitchen.

Llama sees his reflection

in the kettle.

His ears droop.

"Oh, where is my tooth?"

he moans.

Mama and Llama visit Nelly Gnu.

They look in her yard.

Llama finds an earthworm.

Llama finds a pretty pebble.

They swing high to look more.

Whee!

Whoopee!

They have fun.

But they don't find Llama's tooth.

Then they visit Luna.

"I found the tooth!" cries Nelly.

"Sorry," says Luna.

"Those are beads for my art."

Mama Llama hugs Llama.

"We'll keep looking," she says.

They visit Daddy Gnu's bakery.

The tooth is not there.

More friends join the hunt.

They go to the park.

They march around
and look for the tooth.

They have fun.

But they don't find
Llama's tooth.

They look in the sandbox.

Harry the Arctic Hare helps, too.

"I found it!" calls Harry.

"But it is only a piece of shell."

Harry gives Llama ice cream to cheer him up.

Then Llama Llama remembers.

"We went to Gram and

Grandpa's house," he says.

There they check the yard
and kitchen.

They don't find Llama's tooth.

Everyone goes back to Llama's

house to look some more.

They find many lost things.

But they don't find Llama's tooth.

Llama is sad at bedtime.

Then he hears music outside.

Gram is playing her flute.

Gram says, "My flute made awful noises tonight.

And when I turned it over, look what popped out!"

Gram hands it to Mama.

It's Llama Llama's tooth!

Then Llama remembers.

He blew on Gram's flute in her

kitchen!

His tooth must have fallen

out then.

Finally, Llama puts the tooth

under his pillow.

In the morning, Llama checks under his pillow.

The tooth is gone, but now there are coins instead.

"Yippee!" he cheers.